THE BASTARD M

The Low-Energy Guide to Climbing up the Corpo......

By Machy Avelli, MBA, PhD, JD, MD, PsyD, DBW

Text copyright © 2016 Machy Avelli and Peter de Graaf

All Rights Reserved

Cover photo is of the last corporate ladder climbed by the author.

It is now located in a junkyard at an undisclosed location.

Fine Print and Disclaimer:

This book is a parody/satire. In spite of its apparent and often evident truths, it is not to be taken seriously. The publisher and author do not hold, claim to hold, want, or need any liability to or guilt-trips from those people who get fired for implementing the advice and doctrines contained in this book at their workplaces.

To…

… All the bastard managers that I've worked for who inadvertently provided raw material for this book.

Other Works by Machy Avelli:

Plato's I've Got Your Apology Right Here!

Stay tuned for Machy Avelli's next book, available in March 2017:

The 33 Laws of Corporate Screw-Ups

CONTENTS

FOREWORD	1
INTRODUCTION	4
THE FUNDAMENTAL TRUTH	12
THE FIRST SUBVERSION	18
THE SECOND SUBVERSION	22
THE THIRD SUBVERSION	27
THE FOURTH SUBVERSION	30
THE FIFTH SUBVERSION	33
WHY THE FIVE SUBVERSIONS WORK	36
WRAP-UP	44
ADVICE	44
EPILOGUE	45

PREFACE

When people want to get more with doing less, many ambitious managers slaving away at cutting-edge companies, such as those from Big-Time CEO Magazine's Top 500 list below, are reaping the benefits from the principles championed in THE BASTARD MANAGER:

A Day Late Express Shipping

Biased Media Corporation

Blankstare Communications

Burger Burner

No, I Can't Hear You Cellular Networks

Oil & Gas Extractors & Spillers

Plastic Surgery Is Us

Pretentious Persons Outfitters

Side Effect Pharmaceuticals

The Uninformed Environmental Protest Group

The University of Bastardized Knowledge

"The executive management team here at Blankstare Communications have continuously benefitted from the principles insisted on in this book. We give this book to all of our promising middle-managers. I personally enjoy watching them use these powerful principles to stick it to their underlings!"

*Gailbreath Blankstare, CEO,
Blankstare Communications*

FOREWORD

FINALLY! The story that follows presents you with a load of what I've learned from my decades of experience in the communications industry and also from my very expensive ivy league education and practice in philosophy, law, surgical medicine, clinical psychology and applied basket weaving about how bastard managers best undermine their subordinates en route to the top of the corporate ladder. With my five doctoral degrees, you can be sure that I know what the hell I'm talking about.

By "undermine", I mean how manager's subvert corporate mission statements and covenants; how they step on their subordinates' toes; how they feel super-smug while doing it; and how they go home at the end of the day and say to themselves in front of their bathroom mirror, "I sure stuck it to my deputy today!"

This tale, *The Bastard Manager*, is but a glimpse in the life of a middle manager in a rut who learns some valuable lessons about how to navigate the murky waters from which the corporate ladder rises out of and up to the promised land of luxurious executive washrooms, big mahogany desks, beautiful secretaries, stock options, and of course, an enormous salary that is inversely proportional to the work he produces and the knowledge he has.

After you've read this book, you will be ready to use the supreme wisdom contained within to ensure that you and your company's inner circle and good-old boy network follow the principal principle in The Bastard Manager's arsenal, given by Confucius' most famous unwritten advice (find out inside).

This story has unfolded itself endlessly for over 2,500 years. Organizations of all types have used the principles within to stagnate productivity while delivering inferior products and services which somehow, amazingly, increase profits, increase unemployment and perpetuate the upward mobility of future executives the world over.

At the office, men, and more recently women too, who have used *The Five Subversions* are promoted more often to positions with higher salaries that require less knowledge and experience. These men and women also report more enjoyment in their work and a greater sense of success by sticking it to their underlings.

In their personal relationships too, significant and insignificant others, newlyweds, and those on first dates and third dates but have yet to reach first base have also used *The Five Subversions* with similar positive results. Even the parents of snotty, acned adolescents have used *The Five Subversions* on their lazy teens and are reaping the benefits of getting them to do more chores, increase stay-at-home punishment time and justify decreases in their teens' weekly allowances.

I have been touched, sometimes literally by a slap on the face, by the numerous people who have told me how on-the-mark the principles in this book are and how much of their lives have been wasted trying to be the good worker while saying, "Why didn't you write this damn book thirty years ago?" Indeed, satisfaction has improved tremendously, both financially and egotistically, for these people by implementing *The Five Subversions*.

As always, people are asked to do a hell of a lot of work for meager pay. And we all know that doing good work breeds a hell of a lot more work. By discovering the secrets contained within this book, you can rise out of the discord of the cube farm, win the fear of your colleagues and lovers and ostracize all your so-called friends as you embark on your maiden voyage up the ladder of success.

I hope you enjoy *The Bastard Manager* as much as I did writing it and that you reap the rewards of employing its message soon while the people you work with are further oppressed and become more disgruntled as they eventually get out of your way and fall off that corporate ladder.

Machy Avelli, MBA, PhD, JD, MD, PsyD, DBW

INTRODUCTION

The Middle Manager

You've seen him. You've seen the run-down middle-aged middle-manager. His bald head is partially covered by a hard-to-look-at comb-over. He always looks angry and dismayed and is often yelling at the top of his lungs at his subordinates. Yeah, you've seen him. This is the middle-manager, who, like the rest of us, was searching in vain for the good life – the easy life. We've all seen him.

He wanted a luxurious private washroom in his own office, with windows, and a big mahogany desk, a beautiful secretary, and stock options. And, of course, he wanted an enormous salary while producing as little work as possible.

His wants had taken him to the far corners of the production pit on the basement floor and all the way up to the top of the Ivory Tower on the eightieth floor.

He had been in the janitor's closet, on the loading docks, in the mail room, in cramped and stuffy conference rooms holding meaningless meetings, in offices with no windows, in wide open cubicle farms with hundreds of desks and not a single barrier to deflect the cacophony of noise and the superb illusion of productivity. But once, only once, had he been in the offices of the company's most prized and powerful executives at the top of the Ivory Tower. And that was only to get a reprimand that lasted no longer than a minute.

He had spoken to many janitors, truck drivers, clerks, fellow paper-pushers, other dilapidated and balding middle-aged middle-managers, and to just a few high-nose head honchos with no more ego than a rock star.

He overheard the whole gamut of chatter about how people were screwing people over left and right and getting promoted after doing it while getting higher salaries and lots of perks and pats on the back on the way up.

He had seen many bastard managers and coworkers whose organizations and departments seemed to muck everything up while they lived the easy life at the office. They took two hour lunches; they called in sick on Mondays after a weekend of partying or on a Friday before partying; they took multiple chain-smoking breaks and held drawn out conversations at the water cooler or coffee pot about who drafted whom in some fantasy sport, who was hooking up with whom in the office and other mind-numbing gossip. All this while he worked his butt off down to the bone with nothing to show for his efforts but a flat ass, gnawed ears and scores of "Needs Improvement" on his performance review year after year.

Yet, somehow, the company more than just stayed afloat. Indeed, they recorded higher and higher earnings each quarter with fat stock prices to boot. The Bastards, as they were known in upper management, were winning and he was losing, badly.

And most of the bastards thought they were damn good at what they did. He thought otherwise. Near the end of another frustrating day, as the middle-manager spoke with some of the bastards, he asked them, point blank:

"Hey guys. What kind of bastard are you?"

They would reply with the usual putting the cock in the word cocky mannerisms – cheesy smirks, chests puffed out, and ambiguous answers, such as:

"I'm a creator of confusion." Or, "I'm a problem maker." And even, "I'm the boss's son so I don't have to do a damn thing."

He caught the whiff of arrogance in the air and it reeked like a bed of roses. The middle-manager wanted to know just how the bastards were pulling it off.

Then, the middle-manager met with the more down-to-earth managers and coworkers who seemed to be perennial losers, like him, and known in upper management as the Schleps. They showed up to the office early, stayed late, ate lunch at their desks while working, and corrected their coworkers' mistakes. They all looked just like him; both the men and the women: overweight, flat-assed, balding and ears gnawed down to the drum.

So, he asked them the same question, point blank:

"What kind of schlep are you?"

They would reply with the usual ass-kissing mannerisms – nervous smiles, chests sunken in, rolled shoulders and drawn out and jittery answers, such as:

"I'm a solution provider to the nth degree." Or, "I'm a problem solver who strives to find the most efficient solution to problems that plague my department." And even, "I'm the boss's nephew so I have to do everything and I do it 80 hours a week."

After these discussions, he found himself pissed all the way off. But, he did find company in his misery. He figured out that most of the managers and coworkers who seemed to be happiest at their jobs were the bastards. They were interested in anything but the work they were hired to do. The schleps, on the other hand, were the most miserable and were only interested in burying themselves in work that no one gave a crap about.

The middle-manager asked himself how he got in this mess to begin with and tried to figure out what he really wanted. He thought hard to find an answer; so hard, in fact, that he got a headache. -

He was confused and dazed and finally said, "Screw it," and left the office early that day and went straight to the bar around the corner from the Ivory Tower. After a few pitchers of beer and mumbling to himself, he finally figured out what it was that he was after.

He yelled at the top of his lungs, "Easy street!" The other drunks in the bar stared at him like he was hell-bent crazy but, he ignored them. He just had an astonishing epiphany – he wanted to do less and earn more. He wanted to be a bastard manager.

But, he quickly turned blue and realized that he had no idea how to become a bastard. After all, he thought himself to be a good person and he never really could be a bastard. So, he drank more beer and, after a few hours and with only one eye open, he drove home.

The next day, the middle-manager arrived at the office over an hour late with a blinding hangover that was obvious to all and received several high-fives from his bastard colleagues who cheered him on. Bewildered and half-smiling, he strode to his windowless office, dropped off his lunch box, flipped on his computer, and then headed for the coffee maker. While pouring himself a cup of the executive gourmet brew, a schlep asked, "Did you get promoted?" He smiled wide and said nothing. Other schleps nearby cursed under their breath and gave scornful hellos and feigned concern for his well-being.

He had smoked a pack the night before at the bar and was running low on his nicotine dosage. So, he walked away and headed to the garage to the smoking area. When he got down to the little oasis tucked away from the dumpsters and the spew of exhaust gas from the street traffic, he found a group of bastards puffing away. Upon seeing him and his blood-shot eyes, they glad-handed him some more as he lit a cigarette.

He told them how he got as drunk as an Irishman the night before and they all laughed with him. As he was finishing his cigarette, he mentioned that he should get back to work. The bastards, sensing a potential new ally in middle-management, started to butter him up and said in concert – "Nonsense!" and handed him another cigarette. Then, they started yapping stories about how they half-assed this job and that assignment and about how they couldn't believe that they got paid to do what they weren't doing. The middle-manager stood in awe and wondered whether they were just yanking his chain. Sensing this, they let him in on a profound secret. They spoke of some supreme bastard, also known as the CBO, the Chief Bastard Officer, who was their inspiration and teacher for their sub-par work ethic.

Intrigued, he went back to his office and phoned the CBO's secretary to request a meeting. To his disbelief, the woman, named Candyass, a fine woman cut from super model genes and with a silky voice that reminded him of a psychic hotline call he once had, connected his call right away.

The middle-manager asked if the CBO wouldn't be so much of a bastard as to grant him a time to meet for some serious career counseling.

The CBO said, in a thick and raspy Texan drawl, "Hell yeah, son. Come on up any time before 3:00 this week. I usually leave the office at 3:30 for my mud massage."

The middle-manager, silently chuckling, said, "Mud massage?" The CBO replied, "Hey, don't knock it until ya've tried it." They agreed to meet first thing the next morning, at ten a.m.

The next day, the middle-manager arrived on-time at the CBO's office but, he had to wait forty five minutes for him to arrive. Upon his arrival, the CBO said to the middle manager, "Howdy, Combover! Yer on time. Good and welcome to the top of the Ivory Tower. Let's go to my office."

They walked into the CBO's lush and spacious office with a gorgeous view of the city and the harbor below. Finely appointed modern furniture filled the space and included an enormous mahogany desk no smaller than the keel of a yacht. On the desk sat the usual ornaments: a pen set, a nameplate with 'CBO' written in large gold letters, a blotter, two large flat screens, but not a single sheet of paper to be found anywhere.

"Sit," the CBO said. "What's goin' on?" he said with a toothy grin that exposed some top-notch dental work.

Combover said, "Thanks for meeting with me. I want to find out how I can get more with less. All the guys in the smoking area said you taught them everything you know. Will you teach me?"

"Well hell, man! I'd be happy to. I get real tired of offerin' unsolicited advice all the time, so it's nice to hear someone ask for it. But, first, I have to make sure that yer worthy of learnin' the secrets and that we can trust ya with 'em."

"Let's go to the copy room. Candyass! Get yer ass in here!" Candyass rushed over. The CBO said, "Plant a wet one on ole Combover here."

Candyass did as instructed, much to the bewilderment and delight of Combover.

The CBO then said, "Now grab his ass and kiss him hard!" She obliged.

Combover gasped as he came up for air and said, "What's the big idea?"

"Leverage, son! Now, I've got a video and pictures of ya and our fine receptionist here in, shall we say, a compromisin' position. It sure would be a shame if these fell into the wrong hands…"

"You mean my wife's hands?"

"Precisely! Ya sure are a quick study, Combover. Now that we know ya won't spill any of our secrets to the schleps, where do ya wanna start?"

THE FUNDAMENTAL TRUTH

Combover took a minute to wipe Candyass's lipstick off his mouth and regain his composure.

"Ok, so I guess the first question I have is, do you hold meetings?"

The CBO replied, "Only when I absolutely have to. Almost every meetin' is an enormous waste of time. Nothin' gets done. And all people wanna do in meetin's is hear 'emselves talk and talk and talk a bunch of damned nonsense. It's also the biggest illusion of work gettin' done ever. So, I hold 'em only when I have to; just to maintain the illusion."

"The illusion?"

"We'll get to that in a bit. What other questions have ya got?"

"Does someone take down action items?" Combover said.

"Ha! Another illusory concept, son! Action items are nothin' but a way for people to feel good about procrastinatin'. I just listen to Joe and Jane jab on about how they'll get their crap done. Then I assign someone to crack the whip on their asses and that's it. Action item lists do nothin' but grow to longer and longer lists; eventually becomin' the focus of the project rather than the damn project itself. And then, people wanna relist the damn actions and create new lists to track 'em. It's a pointless circle of delay, and potential death, for any project."

Combover started taking notes but, the CBO stopped him.

"Son, don't ever take notes! It's a sure-fire way of gettin' roped into doin' work that ya don't have to. Those middle-manager idiots down there on the fortieth floor, no offense, take notes all the damn time. They make note after note, compile their notes, rewrite 'em, and have their secretaries type 'em up as if they'll ever read 'em. And even if they do read 'em, it's like readin' yesterday's newspaper – nothin' but old news. Those are the same idiots who make action item lists and feed 'em with more crap as they grow to longer lists."

"Man," Combover said, "you sure are perceptive."

"Damn straight, son. I wouldn't be up here on top of the Ivory Tower if I didn't know how to see through the smoke and ignore my damn own reflection in the mirror."

Perplexed, Combover asked, "So, what is your job then if it's not to manage people with meetings and produce results?"

"Damn good question, son! My job is to make my people create confusion. I make sure to confuse the hell outta the customers, my employees, and the board of directors and to anyone who tries to get in the way of me havin' a good ole time!"

Combover said, "I see. So then, you're less of a people person and more of an operations person, right?"

The CBO's jaw dropped and he said, "Son, are ya on crack? I can't confuse operations, can I? I need *people* to confuse! If I confuse the people, then they will seek clarification and also alleviation and relief from their confusion. People hate confusion so much that they'll pay almost anythin' to get outta it. And that's where corporate results come from – in the form of huge piles of cash from alleviatin' people's confusion. Have a look at this, son."

The CBO handed the middle-manager a large white coffee mug with an imprint on it.

He said, "The imprint on this mug is the fundamental truth to help ya get all that ya want. I drink from this damn cup every day to remind me of it. I'll drink coffee outta it, or coffee with liquor, or just plain ole liquor. Never beer, though, since it doesn't mix very well with coffee stains. And sometimes, I'll even drink tea outta it when my executive admin, with whom ya just had the pleasure of neckin' with, is up for tea time."

Combover took hold of the large white coffee mug, which had a strong scent of alcohol engrained in the porcelain, and read the imprint. In large capital letters with hundred dollar bills wrapped around them, it said:

CONFUSION CREATES CASH!

The CBO said, "Think about that for a moment. While ya do, I'm gonna make me a drink. Ya want one?"

Combover was surprised to hear himself say, "Sure."

The CBO got up and poured them each a glass of a fine single malt Scotch on the rocks.

He said, "When yer that hungover, it's hair of the dog all the way."

Combover blushed and said, "How did you know?"

"Hell son, if ya wanna get good at lyin', ya've gotta do a lot more of it. Besides, I could smell ya before I even got off the damn elevator." He snorted a loud chuckle and slapped Combover hard on the back and sat down.

The CBO continued, "Ok, where were we? Oh yeah. Confusion creates cash. In my vast experience, there seems to be two kinds of people in the corporate world – bastards and schleps. Let's start with the bastards. Now, Bastards don't give a damn about anythin' but, they give the illusion that they do. Often times, anyway.

"Schleps, on the other hand, seem to give a damn about everythin'. They wanna save the world and want everyone to know that they're doin' it."

Combover nodded in agreement and prided himself for coming to a similar conclusion before going to the bar the night before. But then, he felt embarrassed and thought that he himself might, in fact, be a schlep.

The CBO continued. "Now, everyone hates bastards. Why is that? Well, it's because they're bastards, that's why! But, also because they've got what every schlep wants: A fancy car, a fancy hairdo, fancy clothes, an attractive partner and of course, a lofty title which bears no damn resemblance to what they do or what they're worth.

"Yull find that all the top management 'round here, includin' the board of directors, and those in close proximity to power are, in fact, a bunch of bastards.

"Yull also find that all the hard workin', stressed-out, save-the-doggone-world workers drive piece of crap minivans and coupes, have bad hair days every day, dress like they endorse consignment shops, have partners who have been whipped by the ugly gene, and most of all, they have bland and borin' titles that no one wants."

Combover raised one eye brow and braced himself.

The CBO said, "Now, which of these two groups do ya find yerself in?"

Combover said nothing.

"That's what I thought! Yer a schlep! But, don't worry, son. Yer seekin' the truth is the first step to fleein' the circus of the schleps. Yer comin' here and askin' for my timeless advice is the first step to stop bein' a clown and to start really managin' 'em!"

Combover tried to squash the sudden of feeling of elation and hope he had ballooning within him. He was so glad he had the minerals to come talk to the CBO.

"Ok, now," the CBO said, "there are five basic principles which, when mastered, will lead ya up the shiny corporate ladder to the promised land; to an office just a little smaller than mine but with all the fine appointments ya see around ya, includin', ya guessed it, yer very own Candyass. I call the collection of these basic principles, *The Five Subversions."*

Combover asked in disbelief, "Subversions?"

"That's right, son. Subversions. Ya know, principles that negate all the phony principles that corporate self-help authors, motivational speakers, and even CEOs are constantly jammin' down people's throats in all-hands meetin's every day. Ya know the ones: Work hard, kiss ass, love yer colleagues in spite of all the personality clashes, come in early, stay late, be magnificent and all that crap. Then one day, right before ya've reached the age of bein' a rickety old man, ya might have saved enough money so that ya can upgrade yer piece of crap minivan to a newer, shinier one, all while yer compromisin' yer health and yer dignity the whole time."

Combover mulled all this over. The CBO was right. In his thirty years of working like a schlep, Combover had nothing to show for it. Neither did any of his colleagues who all sat together every day after work, drowning their corporate complaints in cheap beer. They had realized that it was the bastards who did little work, if any, and they were the ones who seemed to effortlessly climb up that enormously tall corporate ladder to the top.

THE FIRST SUBVERSION

The CBO said, "Ok, Combover, so now that ya understand that confusion always, and I mean always, creates cash, yer ready for *The First Subversion*. What do ya think it is?"

Combover scratched his head.

The CBO said, "Damn son, perhaps I misjudged ya."

Combover said meekly, "Create confusion?"

"That's right! Nice save, son. Create confusion. And what's the best way to create confusion?"

Combover scratched his head again.

"Look son, never scratch yer head in front of other people; especially not in front of yer superiors. Instead, scratch yer chin, very lightly, to show that yer thinkin' but also, that ya still got control."

Combover said, "Provide misinformation when requested?"

"That's right. Except, don't do it only when requested. Anytime ya have to submit a report, provide status, or whatever; just be sure to misinform the receiver."

Combover said, "You mean lie?"

"Hell no, son! Never lie; not outright anyways. Just give incomplete information or information that helps to deviate folks from the objective."

"How do I know what the objective is?"

"Hell, son. What do ya think? The objective of the report, of the status update, of whatever."

Combover's face was cast in confusion.

"I see that yer a bit confused. This would be a good opportunity for me to make some money, now wouldn't it?"

Combover raised both eyebrows.

"Ha! Just kiddin', son. Let me give ya an example."

The CBO reached over to his speaker phone. "Candyass! Get Simmons from Production on the line."

A minute later, Simmons was on the line and, with his funny Yankee accent, he said, "Hello. Simmons is on the line."

"Simmons! CBO here. What's the status of the production cycle on the Francon job?"

The sound of shuffling papers echoed through the phone while Simmons let out a few short bursts of the *I-don't-know-what-the-hell-I'm-doing* whistle.

The CBO, now impatient, said, "Never mind, Simmons. I found it."

"Sure thing boss, is there anything else I can…" The CBO hung up the line.

"See there, Combover? That's a schlep. He's always nervous and he's always ready to kiss my ass. And, he always acts like he could do other things for me when he ain't done what I originally asked him to do."

Combover nodded.

The CBO got back on the speaker phone. "Candyass! Get me Rodriguez on the phone."

A minute later, Rodriguez answered the phone in his slight Tex-Mex accent, "Howda. Rodriguez is here."

"Rodriguez! CBO here. What's the status of the production cycle on the Francon job?"

Rodriguez said confidently, "I have that information right here. It appears that we're on schedule."

"Ok, thanks." The CBO hung up the phone.

"See there, Combover? That's a bastard. I'm pretty damn sure that we're not on 'schedule' but, he played it perfectly. He said what I wanted to hear and accordin' to his schedule, we may very well be on track which means my version of the schedule is probly outta whack. That also means that I'm confused. So now, I've gotta go find the project manager to clear it up. That person will need work overtime to find out the right answer. And there ya have it son, confusion creates cash."

Combover was amazed.

The CBO continued, "Rodriguez is my best production manager. He got a bonus at the end of last quarter that's almost as big as yer salary."

Combover fumed to himself.

"Don't fume, son. Harder truths will be comin' yer way so hold on to yer hat."

"No problem, Chief. I can handle it."

"That's the spirit, son.

"So now that ya've heard *The First Subversion*, what do ya think?"

Combover replied, "It appears that I have to know what I'm talking about but, I don't have to be so accurate about it."

"Son, it is a glorious day. That's absolutely correct. If ya give the impression that ya know what yer talkin' about, even if ya don't, yull impress those with the power to bump ya up that ladder to the promised land. It seems to be gettin' a little shorter, now, don't it?"

Combover nodded enthusiastically.

"Ok, good. And now it's time for *The Second Subversion*."

THE SECOND SUBVERSION

The CBO said, "Now, ya can create confusion all ya want. But, a good way to get people motivated is to concoct an illusion. Plus, ya can't just blabber a bunch of nonsense and hope to rise to the top. The illusion ya concoct has gotta be deceptive but believable, and most importantly, it's gotta be related to the job on yer plate."

Combover nodded in understanding and said, "So, *The Second Subversion* is to concoct meaningful illusions?"

"That's right, son. We all know that illusion is necessary. Look at advertisin'. Have ya ever seen an advertisement on the flat tube for a burger, like the ones they got over there at Burger Burner? Now, those are damned good burgers but, do they ever look like the ones on TV?"

"Never."

"Nope. Not ever. The ones on the screen are the sexiest lookin' burgers ever. They're thick and juicy mouth-waterin' burgers that would make a vegetarian question their lifestyle choice. It looks so good that ya speed on down to the nearest Burger Burner drive-thru, order one or more with some thousand calorie fries and diet soda to delude yerself inta feelin' better about all the calories yer gulpin' down. Then, ya squeal yer car over to the closest parkin' spot. Then what? Ya unwrap the package and find two mushed buns with a slice of meat no thicker than yer dumbphone. It still tastes awfully good but, the aesthetic quality is nowhere close to what was depicted on the tube, right?"

"That's right, Chief."

"So, the illusion here was that of a sexy burger that was so sexy that it made ya run out and go buy one. If they had shown that mushed bun and thin slice of meat, nobody would ever buy 'em. Thus, the illusion was necessary to sell the burger."

Combover nodded in agreement and felt a hunger pang go off in his stomach.

"I bet yer hungry now, ain't ya, Combover?"

"I sure am."

The CBO hit the speaker button and yelled into the phone.

"Candyass! Order me and Combover here some burgers and fries and full-fledged cola from Burger Burner and have 'em delivered."

"Right away, Chief."

"Ok, now let's see how this works in our great company Blankstare Communications."

The CBO got back on the phone. "Candyass! Get Wang from marketin' on the phone."

A minute later, Wang got on the line and in his Americanized Chinese accent and lexicon devoid of articles and plurals said, "Wang is on phone."

"Wang! CBO here."

"Yes, sir."

"I've got a question for ya. How can we increase sales of our dumbphones?"

"Well sir, our sale pretty good right now but, what could do is advertise latest Consumer Advocate report on safety of product. Then…"

"Thanks Wang!" The CBO hung up the phone.

"Ya see that, Combover? Ole Wang there has no clue about illusion. Safety? Who gives a hoot about safety on a doggone cell phone?"

Combover guessed aloud, "No one?"

"That's right, son. No one!

"Now, let me show ya a guy who knows a thing or two about illusion."

The CBO got back on the phone. "Candyass! Get Hammerschmidt from marketin' on the line."

A minute later, Hammerschmidt got on the line and, with his thick Saxony accent, said, "Ja. This is Hammerschmidt on the line here. Ja."

"Hammerschmidt! CBO here. How can we increase sales of our dumbphones?"

"Ja. What we can do is let us make a TV commercial that shows two sexy bikini women talking to each other on our phones on either side of a red expensive German sports car. Ja. We play it like they don't know that they are talking to the other but, they really are, actually. It doesn't matter, no, because, if sexy women are holding the phones they are, then they must be good phones because everyone knows that if you are sexy, you are smart too. Ja."

"Bam! Make it happen, Hammerschmidt!" The CBO hung up the phone.

"Ya see that? Hammerschmidt was all about concoctin' the illusion. Viewers of that ad will see the sexy women holdin' our dumbphones but, they'll be confused as to why they are on either side of the same damn sexy sports car talkin' to each other. To figure it out, they'll go out and buy our phones and bam! Sales go up."

Combover was astonished. He thought of how many times he bought some piece of crap he didn't need only because a bikini-clad woman was pictured next to it. Indeed, he thought, illusion is powerful.

"But, why is it necessary?" Combover said.

The CBO said, "Because, people don't give a crap about the truth. Except for, ya know, the die-hard journalist who, with nothin' better to do, chases stories that lead to his or her untimely death. Mostly though, people don't want the truth because the truth hurts. Instead, they want the image; they want the illusion."

Combover was beginning to understand and said, "So, what you're saying is, produce an image, or an illusion, and the people will be drawn to it like a moth to the flame of a candle."

"Son, I am impressed. That's exactly right. Now, applyin' *The Second Subversion* to the workplace, ya concoct the illusion to yer subordinates that there are massive deadlines that everyone has to work hard to meet and to kiss yer flat ass and tell ya what ya wanna hear and so on. In reality, there're really only a few deadlines in any production company that anyone gives a hoot about. The rest of those deadlines are fabrications to keep workers obedient. Nothin' but illusions."

Combover asked, "Ok, then, how do you keep productivity at efficient levels?"

"Excellent question, son. That leads us to *The Third Subversion*."

THE THIRD SUBVERSION

The CBO said, "The key to efficiency, whether in production, sales, whatever, is to make mountains outta molehills in the name of efficiency and take credit for the solution that anyone might come up with."

Combover said, "I understand but..."

The CBO interrupted and said, "Son, I know what yer gonna ask. Now, I'm gonna let ya in on another important secret. Efficiency is the biggest four-letter word in the corporate world. Most CEOs think that efficiency is gettin' more for less. Ya know, more productivity for less resources; more hours for less pay. And most workers enslaved to the cube farms and windowless offices fall for that line of crap like Gullible George. Efficiency is not the answer. The answer to productivity is good ole problem creation and intimidation, not any damn praisin' or glad-handin' or any of that feel-good garbage. Besides, it's always better to be feared than loved.

"And ya intimidate by makin' mountains outta molehills. Every unforeseen production problem, even the seemin'ly obvious ones that are never accounted for, no matter how many times an 'experienced' manager has done it, planned it and scheduled it, whatever, these problems always have a way of comin' up. When they do, it's yer chance to be a bastard manager and get yer underlin's to solve the problem while ya take the credit.

"Now, some managers, the schelppy ones especially, will say that the underlin' that solved the problem deserves the credit. Well, guess the hell what? The underlin' is the one who gets the promotion while the manager stays on the lower rungs of the ladder and throws a hissy-fit.

"Let me show ya." The CBO got back on the speaker phone and said, "Candyass! Get Avelli on the phone."

Candyass got Avelli on the phone.

Avelli, in his thick old school Italian accent said, "Avelli is on the phone here."

"Avelli! CBO here. Question for ya. What happened to the order of replacement antennae for the Ivory Tower Cell Phone Tower Project?"

"Sir. Oh my goodness, sir, you won't believe what happened. The shipment was delayed because our engineering intern stupidly cancelled the order. I have my people working feverishly to come up with replacements for the installation day next week."

"Ok, Avelli. Keep up the good work." The CBO hung up the phone and smiled wide at Combover.

"Did ya see that? He made a big ole mountain outta little tiny molehill. The antennae are one of the last damned things to be installed on a cell phone tower. And they won't need to be installed on this project for weeks. So, what Avelli did there was make a mountain outta molehill and blamed someone else for the so-called problem that was nothin' more than me askin' for status. He'll get the fabrication company to senselessly expedite another delivery and then he'll take all the credit for it."

Combover nodded and then asked, "What happens to the engineer who made the mistake?"

"Good question, son. The answer to that leads us straight to *The Fourth Subversion*."

THE FOURTH SUBVERSION

The CBO said, "*The Fourth Subversion*, son, is to backstab yer underlin's."

"Backstab?"

"Hell, son, are ya deaf? Why do ya make me repeat everythin' I say? That's such a schlep thing to do. That's right. Backstab! Throw 'em under the bus. In other words, blame 'em, betray 'em, whatever ya wanna call it, for the problem. This subversion is especially effective. Any time yer employees ain't livin' up to yer standards of excellence, wait for that big smelly city bus to come rollin' around the corner, push the schlep in its path, and get outta the way of the splatter."

Combover laughed and the CBO joined him.

The CBO continued, "But seriously, as a bastard manager, and in spite of what everyone tells ya, ya can't take responsibility for somethin' ya have no control over. So, when somethin' goes all hog wild, backstab someone below ya on the ladder, blame 'em for the problem or issue, make 'em come up with a solution and then take the credit."

Combover was aghast. He couldn't believe that after all these years, he was taking crap for his underlings' poor performance and then fixing the problem himself. After all, his title was manager, not worker.

Combover asked, "Could you give an example?"

"Sure, son. Remember when Wang fumbled that answer earlier?"

"Yes, of course."

"If that was ya askin' the question and he gave that answer, yer next step would have been to include that fact in yer weekly report, the one that most people never read, by sayin' somethin' like yer department mishandled the situation or in some way that's not too harsh but, casts a negative shadow."

Combover replied, "If no one reads the reports, what difference will it make?"

"It'll make all the difference in the world when it's performance review and forced rankin' time. Most managers and executives don't read reports. Nor do they remember mediocre achievements. What they do remember though, is both big sales that make a lotta money and big screw ups that cost us a buncha money."

"Understood. So, in other words," Combover asked, "the people who do the work, and the people who screw it up, they are the ones responsible for it."

"Ya got it, son!"

"So, after I've created confusion, concocted meaningful illusions, made mountains out of molehills and then backstabbed my underlings, what's next?"

"Good question, son. The next and final step to yer enlightenment is *The Fifth Subversion*."

THE FIFTH SUBVERSION

The CBO continued and said, "*The Fifth Subversion*, son, is to renege on promises."

Combover tried to keep a poker face on his astonishment. He was never any good at poker.

"Now, son, stick with me here. And, by the way, learn how to play some poker before ya try to pull that face again."

Combover said, "Texas Hold'em?"

The CBO said, "Of course, son. What else is there?

"Now look. People love promises. Of course, they love when the promises are fulfilled but, if ya make the promise, break it with some crafty excuse that sounds like it was for the better of the company or to save money or some other load of malarkey and they'll usually let ya off the hook."

Combover said, "Why would I do that?"

"Do what?"

"Renege on a promise I've made?"

"I'm glad ya asked, Combover, because, once ya've made the promise, nearly always, somethin' will happen causin' ya to have to break it. Renegin' on the promise opens the door to cycle back to *The First Subversion* to cover yer tracks."

"Brilliant," Combover said under his breath.

"That's right, son. It is brilliance."

"So, Avelli employed this principle perfectly on the phone just a minute ago. He promised to get the antennae to the site by next week. Now, I know for a fact that that won't happen. But, he made the promise and that's what big dogs like me wanna hear. Promises and results. Have ya ever heard of a big dog hearin' what he didn't wanna hear?"

"Who hasn't?"

"Exactly. Of course ya have. Everybody has. But, what most people don't realize is that when someone reports to the big dog what he doesn't wanna hear, that person usually gets fired or at least, gets their ear chewed on so badly, it'll look like a Rottweiler's chew toy."

Combover raised his eyebrows to where his hairline once was.

"Don't go soft on me now, Combover. That's the nature of the business. Ya gotta get used to it if ya wanna be a bastard manager."

Combover shrugged and relaxed. He thought to himself that he could handle this. He just couldn't believe that it was this easy to move up the corporate ladder and to get on easy street.

He then asked the CBO, "So, why do *The Five Subversions* work?"

WHY THE FIVE SUBVERSIONS WORK

The CBO said, "Yet another excellent question, son. Let me show ya by way of example.

"Do ya ever go to the bar, to the movies, to the mall, anywhere outside of work on the weekends?"

"Sure."

"Of course ya do. In those arenas, the two kinds of people we've discussed and that ya see at those places on a Saturday afternoon, they're generally happy. Why? Because they don't have some middle manager breathin' down their necks. But, if ya go on Sunday afternoon, most of the schleps ya see have an anxiety about havin' to go back to work after a measly two days off. On the other hand, the bastards ya see, they're still happy as clams and are excited to get back to work. Why? Because, it's a new week and a chance to apply *The Five Subversions* again. It's the same thing, week after week. It's like a competition among 'em – to see who can come up with the greatest, most profound application of *The Five Subversions*. It is an incredible motivator to go socialize with yer work friends, come up with ways to deceive and stick it to their underlin's."

Combover asked, "Doesn't this get to a point where a company can fail?"

"Sure does. But, companies fail all the time. The best companies, a company like Blankstare Communications, stay alive and prosper because we value both the bastards and the schleps. And, almost always, it's the bastards that rise up the corporate ladder because they know how to get people to do the work. Hell, the schleps don't know how to get 'emselves to do work. But, be warned, ya don't show that value too often to the schleps otherwise, they get needy and become drama queens. It's not a perfect system, but it's one that's worked well in my thirty five years in the business."

Combover nodded and asked, "How so, exactly?"

The CBO said, "Well, son, the bastards concoct the illusion to upper management that they know how to get things done. And they do it while not workin' any harder than they have to.

"The schlep mentality is to work hard and if they get chewed out or reprimanded somehow, they think it's best to keep their heads low, not make waves and kiss the boss's ass and then they'll be safe. Everyone wants security. It's only the bastard managers that realize that achievin' security takes risk. And the risk in this case is simply not obeyin' the standard model of the schlep.

"Here's another example that'll maybe help ya understand.

"Suppose ya have a rat in a maze. If yer the rat, what's yer objective?"

Combover thought the question over for a moment and then said, "To get out of the maze."

"That's right, son. He doesn't wanna be in a maze so, he'll skedaddle through the maze and bump into walls and corners until he finds his way out, which can take a hell of a long time.

"Suppose now we put some food at the exit of the maze, say a piece of good ole aged Swiss cheese. Now, the rat has even more motivation and incentive to get outta the maze, right?"

Combover nodded in agreement.

"Not only that, but the good ole aged Swiss cheese has an odor that's particularly strong and well suited to the rat's sense of smell. Now, the rat has a direction to head to. He has a purpose. He smells the cheese and makes his way through the maze in record time to find the cheese at the end of the maze."

"Amazing," Combover said.

"Not really, but I think I know what ya mean. The point of this example is that employees on the lower rungs of the ladder are like rats. They're caught in a maze and are always bumpin' into walls and corners and even each other as they try to get outta the maze and into a better maze known as middle management."

Combover said, "That's exactly how I felt when was in the cube farm."

"I knew ya would appreciate the analogy. The problem is that the Swiss cheese at the end of the maze isn't really there. No siree. In fact, there ain't nothin' there but an illusion. Do ya remember *The Second Subversion*?

Combover said proudly, "I sure do. Illusion is necessary."

"That's right, son. So, the illusion that upper management has placed at the end of the maze, the one that the lower rung employees find 'emselves caught in all the time gives off a false scent. That scent directs the rat to the end of the maze. But, lo and behold, by the time the schlep thinks he got there, the smell is gone and, as usual, he finds himself in another and even bigger maze with, ya guessed it, another false scent. And again, as I've said many times already, the schlep bounces off the walls, keeps goin' in circles and ain't never able to exit the maze. There are few exceptions of course but, for most schleps, that's how it is.

"But, the bastards, they have a tremendous sense of smell and that's the smell of easy street. They don't need no stinkin' cheese to guide 'em to their goal of gettin' outta the maze. The smell of easy street is one that can be visualized and we all know the power of visualization, don't we?"

"We sure do."

"Not only that, the bastard knows how to levitate himself, so to speak, above the maze and see his way out. It may take a while, for no bastard can exit the maze too quickly since there is some value to startin' off in the schlep ranks and then movin' up. Whereas the true schlep, he's too busy with his nose to the grindstone to see the layout of the maze. He's too busy keepin' his head down to see the big picture."

Combover was amazed at the CBO's brilliance.

"Ya've heard of the expression, 'See the forest through the trees?'"

"I have."

"Good. The bastards know how to see the forest and every once in a while, they can't help to stop to look at the bark of the tree in front of 'em. But, they stay true to their goal which is to focus on the forest and the tallest trees."

"Why is that?"

"Because that's where he can set up his ladder to climb to the top!"

Combover nodded vigorously and he visualized himself climbing high on that ladder.

"Ya see, everyone thinks there's only one corporate ladder. Hogwash! There are many corporate ladders in any doggone corporation. All ya have to do is find one that ya can use or else, bring yer own damn ladder and start climbin'."

Combover was taking all this in and it was starting to gel in his mind.

The CBO then pointed to a large framed picture on the far wall from his desk.

"Ya see that picture over yonder?"

"Yes. It's a picture of a forest."

"Yes, but it ain't just any forest. It's the Amazon forest, the second largest forest in the whole doggone world. How many trees are in that forest?"

"I don't know. Millions?"

"I don't know either but, the correct answer is that ya don't care. It's a forest! This tree or that tree don't matter because as soon as it does matter, yer lost, just as if ya were a rat in the maze."

"All this is great sir but, it sounds to me like in order to get to the top, you have to be manipulative. Doesn't moral society hate manipulators?"

"Son, it's just as true as longhorns havin' long horns. Let me ask ya this. Do ya care what moral society says or thinks?"

"Not really."

"Good. How many people in the world manipulate others?"

"I don't know. Not too many, I guess."

"Wrong, Combover! Everyone manipulates! Manipulation has been goin' on since the first cave couple were settin' fires and decidin' how to cook burgers outta the woolly mammoth they had just done hunted down. The only people that hate manipulation are the ones that get manipulated because they always say to 'emselves after realizin' they've been manipulated: 'I shoulda known better' or 'how could I not have seen that comin'? People who are successful at manipulation are the ones who rise to the top."

"I feel as though I'm being manipulated here."

"Ha! Of course ya are, son. But yer benefittin' from this manipulation ain't ya?"

"Yes, sir."

"And, I am too. Manipulation, as most people can't realize, don't have to be no zero sum game. It can be win-win. However, if ya use honesty too much, like the schleps usually do, then what happens?"

"Others can see them coming from a mile away."

"Son, that is absolutely correct. Have ya ever heard of Machiavelli?"

"No, sir."

"He was an Italian politician from over four hundred years ago and probly, the father of political science. Do ya know what political science is all about?"

"Manipulation?"

"Son, I see a bright future for ya around here. That's exactly right. And that plays heavily in to life in the corporate world. Here is one of my favorite Machiavelli quotes:

"Never attempt to win by force what can be won by deception."

Combover nodded appreciatively.

The CBO said, "Ok son, that's it. Ya now have the secrets to success. Now, bear in mind that these principles only apply to yer underlin's! If ya try to pull any of this crap at the executive level, yull be outta here faster than ya can say golden parachute."

"Understood, sir!"

Combover got up to leave and was about to give gratitude to the CBO for the invaluable lessons he had heard.

The CBO said, "Oh and son, one last bit of advice for ya."

"Sir?"

"Get rid of that awful comb over. Shave yer head or grow yerself some ear pointers."

"Yes, sir. Thank you, sir."

Combover was very excited and went back to his office with a spring in his step he hadn't felt since he lost his virginity. In spite of the CBO's advice, he quickly wrote some notes on what he had learned, as follows:

WRAP-UP

The Five Subversions:

1. Create confusion
2. Concoct meaningful illusions
3. Make mountains out of molehills
4. Backstab underlings
5. Renege on promises

ADVICE

The CBO's timeless tips:

1. If you want to get good at lying, you have to do a lot more of it.
2. Never scratch your head in front of your colleagues or superiors.
3. Learn how to play poker.
4. See the forest through the trees.
5. Never attempt to win by force what can be won by deception.
6. Get rid of the comb-over.

EPILOGUE

After his meeting with the CBO, he started hitting the gym and in less than two years, he had lost eighty pounds of blubber. Twice a week, he baked himself in a tanning bed to get that bronzed executive look. After practicing *The Five Subversions*, Combover, now known as Cue Ball, was promoted to executive Vice President, serving directly under the CBO and was making over three times the salary he was at before he visited the CBO. He had the big mahogany desk, a beautiful secretary named Sweetpants, his own executive washroom and most importantly, the fear and respect of his underlings.

How did he do all of this in such a short time?

Because, he diligently practiced *The Five Subversions*: He created confusion; he concocted meaningful illusions, he made mountains out of molehills; he stabbed his underlings in the back as he patted them on their shoulder from the front; and he reneged on the seemingly most promising promises.

The confusion he created made him piles of cash; cash that went to his bank account and added to the company's bottom line. His illusions created motivated schleps. His mountains of problems made from molehills sparked innovation. His back stabbings created loyalty and his reneged promises led to mass layoffs of the deadwood at the company. To show his gratitude and appreciation, he paid it forward to the next up-and-coming bastard manager, a guy named Hairpiece.

THE END

Printed in Great Britain
by Amazon